This Book Belongs To:

....

Aged: ....

BOOK 1
In the series

To **Read** & **Colour** In

This book has been designed so that once you have read it you can carefully colour in each picture with pencil crayons.

for big kids and little kids

The Wizard

Of

Worsley Woods

By

P.G. Wilson

1. THE WIZARD

No one knew about the Wizard of Worsley Woods, he kept himself to himself, hidden away from all the other people of the world. He was shy, as wizards tend to be, and he didn't like lots of people and the fuss they brought. So he hid in the far corners of the woods, away from all the dog walkers and families and children that went there for walks.

His favourite times where when the wood was empty; when all the children were at school, or at dusk and dawn, or when the weather was really bad. Then he could wander around wherever he wanted without the fear of being spotted. So if you ever go to

Worsley Woods you won't see him, but he might see you!

His name was Wendell the Wizard of Worsley Woods and it was his job to look after all the animals, the birds and the bees and all the trees and plants and flowers and everything that lived there. He kept the hobgoblins away and an eye on the fairies. He picked up litter, that foolish people had dropped, and he put it in the bin for them. He hated litter because it made the woods look awful and it could be a danger to the animals.

He had a grey beard and wore a pointed wizard's hat and a cloak, which were both blue. His home was a tree house on the edge of the wood, so hidden that you would never find it.

2. THE LOST HEDGEHOG

Early one morning the wizard was walking through the woods when he heard someone calling out. It was his friend Robin Redbreast, a little bird he had known for a long time.

"Wizard, Wizard! Come this way!" yelled the robin.

"Whatever is the matter, twittering so loudly, so early in the morning?" asked the wizard.

"Follow me," said the robin and it flew off down the path and the wizard followed it to a patch of brambles where something was rustling about on the floor amongst the leaves.

"It is this little hedgehog," said the robin flying over it.

The wizard looked down and saw a hedgehog with a cup over its head.

"He must be very thirsty," said the wizard.

"He's not thirsty; he has the coffee cup stuck on his head. I have been trying to pull it off but I can't. Please can you help?" asked the robin.

"Of course I can," he replied and he bent down and pulled the coffee cup off the hedgehog's head.

"Oh thank you so much," said the hedgehog with a smile.

"How did you get that stuck on your head?" asked the wizard.

"In the night when it was dark, I was snuffling about the leaves when I accidentally walked into it," explained the hedgehog.

"I hate litter. When will people learn that they should not drop their litter!" said the angry wizard.

Then he pulled a bag out of his cloak and put the coffee cup in it so he could put it in the litter bin later on.

"So what is your name young hedgehog?" asked the wizard.

"Pricklebob," he replied.

"I haven't seen you in these woods before."

"No, I came here a few days ago, across the busy road."

"You should know better than to be crossing roads. Roads are not a place hedgehogs should be crossing," the wizard told him.

"I had to cross the road, I was leaving home. I lived in a garden but one day workmen turned up and started digging up the earth so

I ran away. Then in the night I got lost and I saw all these trees here and I ran across the road as fast as I could. Can I come and live here?" asked the hedgehog.

"Of course you can live here. You have had a worrying time, but you are perfectly safe here, apart from the odd coffee cup. Welcome to Worsley Woods. My name is Wendell the Wizard of Worsley Woods," he said then he bent down and shook the little hedgehog's paw and asked, "Have you had any breakfast yet?"

"No, I am very hungry," replied the hedgehog sadly.

"Would you like to come for some breakfast with me?"

"Yes please!" said the hedgehog.

"Then follow me to my tree house on the other side of the wood," said the wizard.

"A tree house, I cannot climb up a tree," said the hedgehog.

"Don't worry Pricklebob, I will carry you up," said the wizard with a smile.

"Can I come too?" asked Robin Redbreast, who was still there watching them.

"Of course you can, the more the merrier," said the wizard.

Then the wizard, the hedgehog and the robin went off down the wooded path to have breakfast at his tree house hidden in the wood...

3. BREAKFAST

The Wizard carried the hedgehog up the ladders and into his tree house. The robin flew up with ease. Then they all sat around his table while he made them a warm breakfast of porridge and honey.

"So why do you live in a tree house?" asked the hedgehog.

"Why not live in a tree house? I like it up here amongst the leaves and when the wind blows at night, the tree sways and rocks me to sleep in my bed," he said.

"I like to live beneath a hedge, snuggled up under the leaves," said the hedgehog.

"I like to live in a nest in a little holly hedge, I feel safe in there. The spiky holly leaves keep intruders away," said the robin.

"Why do you live in the woods and not in a town like all the other people?" the hedgehog asked the wizard.

"Because it is my job to live in the woods and look after all the animals," he explained.

"Why is it your job?"

"Because the Green Man gave me the job to look after this wood and all its animals, as my father did before me," said the wizard.

"Who is the Green Man?" asked Pricklebob.

"Oh just some old chap covered in leaves."

"What are you up to for the rest of the day?" asked the robin, who was rather curious.

"I have to go and see an injured rabbit that lives down by Woods End on the Cow Fields," replied the wizard.

"In the afternoon in broad daylight, someone might see you," said the robin fretfully.

"I will be careful, I am rather good at hiding amongst the trees and bushes," he said.

"But you have to cross a road to get there," warned the robin.

"I don't like roads," said the hedgehog nervously.

"Nor do I but I have no choice, I promised I would go and I stick to my word. The rabbit has a wounded foot, cut on some barbed wire and I really must go," said the wizard.

After their breakfast, the wizard helped the hedgehog back down from his tree house and let him go on his way, to snuffle around and explore his new home in the wood. The robin flew off to look for grubs in the warm afternoon and the wizard set off to the Cow Fields at Woods End...

4. THE RABBIT'S FOOT

Down the secret winding woodland paths the wizard walked. This way and that, he made his way down to 'The Lake' as he called it, but others knew it as Old Warke Dam.

There were some people walking dogs about so he hid behind a few bushes until they were gone. They didn't see him at all but the dogs knew he was there. They could smell him but they had no interest in him.

When they had gone the wizard nipped by the lake, down the path passed the lodge house near where the badgers lived, and then to the Wild Flower Path that led down to

16

Woods End. This path was always much quieter than others because it was forever muddy, and people tend to avoid the muddiest areas. It was less busy but it went by a school, so he had to make sure the children were not out in the playground, or he might be seen. Along this trail grew many wild flowers and plants, especially towards the end where in spring there grew lots of wild garlic.

At the end of the path it sloped down to a road where the cars and the trucks rushed through at great speed. He didn't like this road because it was where he might be seen. When he'd looked each way, and listened, and was sure nothing was coming, he carefully crossed the road.

On the other side was a cottage with a thatched roof and down by the side of that a little rough road. This was the Woods End, so called because this last bit of woodland was where Worsley Woods ended.

Down through the old trees he walked until he came to a fence and the wide area of green grass spread out before him. It was the Cow Fields and from here he could see for a long way, across the grassland that went all the way to the busy Monton Green village and its church spire, over a mile away.

There by the gate to the fields he hung around for a moment until one of the rabbits saw him and said, "Wizard come this way," and he followed the little rabbit across the grass to some holes to their warren by the north edge of the pasture. There he knelt down near the rabbit hole and slowly out limped a very unhappy looking young rabbit with a sore foot.

"Tell me what the matter is?" the wizard asked the rabbit.

"I trod on some rusty barbed wire that was left by the side of the field and now my foot hurts," the rabbit replied.

"Well let me see what I can do for you," said the wizard and he looked at the rabbit's injured foot. From his pocket he got some cream and carefully rubbed it on the wound. After that he got a little bandage and wrapped it round the rabbit's foot, tying it on tightly so that it didn't slip off.

"Thank you wizard," said the rabbit, which was very glad of his care and attention.

"It is what I do," said the wizard with a smile.

Then the rabbits said goodbye and crept back down into their burrows and deep into the warren. They didn't like being above ground in the afternoon in the bright daylight.

The wizard got up from his knees and made his way back across the field to the path to go home. Just at that time a girl and a boy were walking nearby with their grandmother and they saw the wizard.

"Who is that strange man over there?" asked the girl.

"I can't see anyone?" said their grandma.

"It's a magician!" shouted the boy.

"It's not a magician it's a wizard," said the girl.

"I can't see him. Are you making this up?" asked their grandma.

"No we're not he is there," shouted the boy pointing to where the wizard had been, but he had mysteriously disappeared.

"Let me put my glasses on," said their grandma and when she put them on and looked, she couldn't see anyone. "There is no one there! You are playing a trick on me."

"No we are not. He was there a moment ago and then he just vanished into the trees," said the girl.

"What did he look like?" asked their grandma.

"He had a pointed hat and he had a grey beard," said the boy.

"Yes and he was old, but not that old, and had a cloak like a wizard," added the girl.

"Oh, you must have seen *him*," said grandma with a smile on her face.

"Seen who?" they both asked.

"The Wizard of Worsley Woods," she told them.

"Who is that?" they asked.

"When I was a little girl, probably younger than you two are today, I saw a wizard in the woods and my grandma told me a rhyme about him," she said.

"What was it?" asked the boy.

"Tell it us then," insisted the girl.

So the grandma told them the rhyme:

"The Wizard of Worsley Woods
He only ever does good
And all the animals know his name
And far and wide they know his fame

The Wizard of Worsley Woods
Helps anyone one he could
He loves the flowers and the trees
And all the birds and all the bees

The Wizard of Worsley Woods
Is never misunderstood
For he is magic and he is kind
The nicest wizard you'll ever find
Is...

The Wizard of Worsley Woods!"

5 GRANDMA

The wizard didn't know he had been seen by the children on the Cow Fields so he didn't worry about it. He'd been seen few times over the years and because it was a rare event, and only a small number of people had actually seen a peep of him, no one ever believed them. However, the children's grandma believed in him because when she was little she had seen the wizard in the wood and her grandma had told her the poem.

It was not the same wizard though. It wasn't Wendell the Wizard of Worsley Wood; it had been Wesley the Wizard of Worsley Wood a long time ago. He was Wendell's dad who had looked after the woods before he had took over.

"Grandma did you really see the wizard when you were little?" asked the girl.

"Yes, just once, but he was very, very old at that time. There's no way the wizard can still be living in the woods. He would be in a wizard's nursing home by now. He'd be over a hundred years old," she explained.

"Maybe it's a new wizard," suggested the girl.

"Does every wood have a wizard?" asked the boy.

"Oh no, only the special woods have a wizard. Some woods have a witch and some woods have fairies. Some bad woods have nasty little hobgoblins in them. All woods have some kind of magic, until they are chopped down. Then their magic disappears. You can of course plant new trees and a new wood, but it takes many years for the magic to return," their grandma told them.

"Grandma, when we come for a walk with you next week can we go and find the wizard in the wood?" asked the boy.

"You will not find him," she said.

"Why not?" asked the girl.

"Because you cannot find a wizard, they are far too good at hiding. They have to hide from people all their lives, so you will never find him," said their grandma and the children looked sad. Then she added, "You can catch him though!"

"How do we do that?" they asked.

"To catch a wizard you need a hot almond cake, a fishing rod and to get up very early in the morning..." said their grandma and the children both looked very confused at her.

"Tell us more," they begged.

So their grandma told them how to catch a wizard, "To catch a wizard you must first get up very early in the morning, even before the sun is awake. This is because wizards avoid people, so they only go out at dusk or at dawn or in the night. Or when there is no one else around. Secondly you need a hot cake; I say almond cake but any nice cake will do. I say almond cake because when it is hot, it smells so strong and good, and the smell wafts across the wood. This will draw him near because wizards love hot cake."

"And why the fishing rod?" asked the boy curiously.

"I was thinking if we put the fishing rod line over a branch of a tree and then we hooked it on to the cake, when the wizard tries to take the cake, we reel in the fishing line and the cake goes up in the air so the wizard can't get it. Then when he is confused we can catch him," said grandma with a grin.

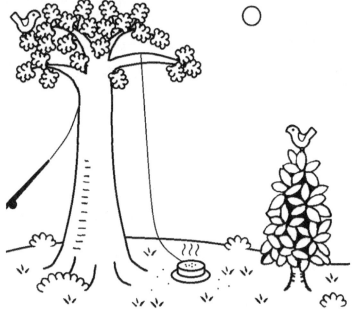

"Wizard fishing!" said the boy.
"That's a great idea grandma, can we do it?" asked the girl.
"No we can't. I was only joking. We can't go wizard fishing its silly!" said their grandma and she refused to have anything to do with it but her grandchildren wanted to do it.

6. WIZARD FISHING

The children didn't see their grandma for another week but in that time they talked of nothing other than going 'wizard fishing'. The boy had got an old fishing rod from a second hand shop and the girl had got an almond cake from the supermarket. All they needed now was to spend the night at their grandma's house because it was near the woods. Then get up really early in the morning and set the cake trap for the wizard... if they could get their grandma to agree to it.

The next weekend they spent a night at their grandma's house and they nagged and badgered and pestered her until she was so irritated with them she agreed, just so she could get some peace.

The next morning they got up out of bed at a quarter to six which was earlier than any of them had ever gotten up before. They couldn't even open their eyes properly and it was still dark outside. Grandma said they were only ever going to try this once because she did not like early mornings at her age.

The boy got his fishing rod and the girl put the almond cake in the microwave to heat it up then put it in a plastic tub to keep it warm. Their grandma brought a plate to put the cake on, so it didn't get dirty on the floor. Then as the dawn was breaking and the sun was just peeping over the horizon they went for a walk into Worsley Woods.

All the birds were singing in the trees and the air was crisp and cold. Grandma led them up to the High Woods because she thought from there the smell of the cake would carry furthest on the morning breeze.

There they found a tree with a suitable branch and the boy flipped the fishing line over it and pulled the hook down. Their grandma put the plate on the ground and the girl opened her plastic tub and put the still warm almond cake on the plate. It smelled delicious.

"Shall we just eat the cake and go home?" asked their grandma.

"No," they told her.

Then they went and hid behind some bushes and waited... and waited... and waited...

Wendell the Wizard of Worsley Woods was just getting up out of his bed when he smelt something sweet in the air. He didn't know what it was at first as his nose was still half asleep. Then as he woke up some more he realised he could smell warm cake, not something you ever smell first thing in the morning in the woods!

"What is this I smell so early in the morning? Cake in the wood, how can this be? I must investigate," he thought to himself.

He jumped up out of his bed, put on his hat and shoes and went out to look for where the delicious smell was coming from.

"I really like cake," he muttered to himself as he sniffed the air to find out the direction it was coming from, and soon he was headed to the High Woods.

The children and their grandma stayed hidden behind some bushes. The morning sun was peering through the trees when they first heard that someone was coming their way. They looked down the path and sure enough it was the Wizard of Worsley Woods in his pointed hat and cloak.

"Here he is," said the boy.

"Yes, grandma it is him," said the girl.

"Shhh shut up the pair of you or you will scare him off," said their grandma and they both froze still with excitement.

Then the wizard came off the path and up the hilly bit into the High Woods where they were waiting...

7. THEY CATCH THE WIZARD

The wizard was almost in a trance and utterly befuddled as to why there was a strong smell of cake in the woods. He walked directly towards the cake and saw it on a plate on the ground and he was astonished.

"What strange witchcraft or pixie trick is this?" he said out aloud but there was no reply. He scratched his chin and murmured for a while and said, "Is this work of a hobgoblin?" but again no one replied.

Then he went over to the cake. Knelt down on the ground and looked at it, sniffed it, then with his fingers pinched a bit of it and put it in his mouth and tasted it and said, "Well it isn't poisoned, in fact it tastes delicious!" then as he tried to pick it up the boy wound the reel on the fishing rod and the cake was pulled up into the sky above him so he couldn't reach it.

"What foul and cruel magic is this?" yelled the angry wizard as the cake dangled about above his head and he tried to grab it.

Then the children and the grandma ran out from behind the bush, they were laughing and shouted, "Surprise! We have caught you!"

The wizard nearly jumped out of his skin in shock and said, "What are you doing trying to trick me with a cake?"

"We wanted to meet you," said the boy and he unwound the fishing line lowering the cake and the wizard grabbed it.

"We wanted to meet the Wizard of Worsley Woods," said the girl.

"But why? No one is even supposed to know about me," he replied.

"Well I know about you and you were seen on the Cow Fields by Woods End last week," said their grandma.

"You did this; you told them how to catch me. I am supposed to stay secret," said the wizard pointing to the grandma.

"They are just children, they mean no harm," said the grandma.

"But what if they tell other people?" said the wizard nervously.

"Other people won't even believe them if they did. No one believes in wizards in the twenty first century anyway," explained the grandma.

"No one believes in wizards because there's not much call for them anymore, what with all the woods being chopped down and the hedges grubbed up to make way for supermarket car parks and housing estates," said the wizard sadly.

"Don't worry mister wizard. We won't tell anyone. We will keep you a secret," said the girl.

"There you go, nothing to worry about," the grandma told him.

"As long as you promise to be our friend, we won't tell anyone," said the boy.

"Be your friend! What!" gasped the wizard.

"They are just children and the school holidays will soon be over. They won't be troubling you for a long time," said their grandma.

"Well I don't know about that... I might just disappear and be more careful. Then no one will believe you. They'll just think you're kids making up stories," he said.

"You can keep the cake if you promise to be our friend," said the girl.

The wizard looked at the cake he held in his hands and sniffed it. It was good. It was better than any cake he had had in a long time and he said, "I don't know, one cake doesn't make a friendship. Will there be other cakes?" he asked.

"Yes, there will be more cakes. Chocolate cakes and cream scones," said their grandma.

"Honestly? Cream scones with jam?" he asked.

"Of course with jam, I am very good at baking," said their grandma.

"Alright then, as long as there will be more cakes, and you promise to keep me secret then I will be your friend for the rest of the school holidays," said the wizard and he shook their hands and added, "but I am not going to tell you where I live because that is the most 'secretist', 'secrety', secret there is and you already know far too much by half. So thanks for the cake and I will have to be off," said the wizard and he started to walk off into the woods.

"Wait, where are you going?" asked the girl.

"I am a very busy man. I have to go and see an owl with a runny nose up by Windy Meadow," he said.

"But how can we see you again?" asked the boy.

"With your eyeballs," he replied.

"No, don't be silly. How can we meet you again?" asked the girl.

"Well if you come to the wood, you won't see me, but I will see you and when I do I will come and talk to you," he said.

"But how do we know you will do that? You might just be lying and they will never see you again," said the grandma.

"Well if I see you and you have cake with you, the chances are you will definitely see me again, but on the other hand, should you not have cake then you probably won't see me at all," explained the wizard and then he said goodbye to them with a friendly smile and walked off into the woods and vanished...

8. WISE OWL

The wizard went to see Owlberta the Wise Owl, because she had a terrible runny nose and wasn't feeling good at all. He went over the bridge near the swampy place and up the little path that led to the Windy Meadow where the owl lived. There he found the huge tall sycamore tree that was its home.

The wizard stood at the bottom of the tree and shouted up to her: "Wise Owl! Wise Owl! Here I am," and waited for a while for it to appear.

Slowly the owl appeared, poking its nose out of its hole and it yelled, "Come up wizard!"

"Can't you come down to me?" asked the wizard.

"But I am ever so ill," she replied.

"Yes but I can't climb all that way up your tree. It's too tall without enough branches to hold on to. It would be much easier if you were to fly down," he said looking up at the owl.

The owl wasn't keen on coming out of her tree hole, but she launched herself off a branch and without effort, glided in a spiral gently down to earth and landed on the grass in front of him. He bent down and allowed the owl to climb onto his arm and he picked her up.

"Now how is your runny nose Owlberta?" asked the wizard.

"It is terrible. My runny nose has become a sniffle and that sniffle is turning into a cold and that cold might turn into the flu," said the owl.

"Oh dear, well, I have brought you some medicine," said the wizard and he took from his pocket a small bottle of the remedy he made for owls with colds.

"Oh I don't want that yucky potion."

The owl pulled its face and turned away in disgust at the medicine.

"I cannot help you if you won't take the cure," explained the wizard.

"I think it would be best if I came and stayed with you at your house, where it is nice and warm by your fire place," said the owl.

"But you only have a sniffle," said the wizard.

"But it might become a cold!" replied the owl.

"Oh all right then, you can come and stay at my tree house while you get better - as long as you agree to take the medicine," said the wizard.

The owl agreed and the wizard took her home to his tree house to look after her. He sat her down on his comfy chair by the warm fire where she was very happy.

"So tell me, how are you Wendell?" the owl asked him after she had got cosy in the chair.

"Oh Wise Owl, I have been seen by people, little people, children as a matter of fact and I don't know what to do," he told her.

"Ah well don't worry about it too much. It happens to the best of us. No one believes the tales children tell. Even I have been seen by people in the woods and us owls are very secretive. Just be a bit more careful next time," she said.

"It's a bit more difficult that. I accidentally agreed to be their friend," he explained.

"Why ever did you do that?"

"I had no choice. They set a trap and caught me with cake."

The owl burst out laughing then said, "So what are you going to do?"

"Hopefully it is only until the end of the school holidays, and they did promise to bring me cakes, so I guess I will just have to be their friends," said the wizard.

"Will the Green Man be annoyed with you for making friends with these little people? You know what the rules are. All wood wizards must keep themselves hidden," said the Wise Owl.

"I think these children won't be any problem. They are still good inside and have not been led to mischief by the world, and as for the Green Man, he won't be bothered about a couple of children, he has his hands full with all that is happening in the world at the moment," said the wizard.

"Ah well there's no point worrying. Worrying never solved a problem, not in my experience. What is done is done. It is what it is, but most importantly of all..." said the owl then she stopped for a moment, as in deep thought.

"What is most important of all?" asked the wizard urgently.

"Most important of all, is that you have some cake, I believe..." said the owl hinting that she wanted some.

"Ah yes, cake," he replied.

So the wizard put the kettle on and made a pot of tea, then cut them both a slice of the almond cake, which they enjoyed very much.

9 THE CHILDREN RETURN

About a week later, early in the morning the wizard was walking through the woods, enjoying the dawn chorus of birdsong and looking for bits of litter as he usually did, when he heard shouting and noise. He sneaked through the forest to see what was going on and there were the children again, up in the High Woods yelling out for him as loud as they could.

"Wizard, wizard, we are here again and we've brought some more cake!" they shouted.

The wizard didn't like them making all that noise so early in the morning and he ran through the wood to them.

"Here he is," shouted the boy.

The wizard jogged through the bushes to them puffing and panting.

"Shut up and stop making such a hullabaloo!" he said to them urgently.

"What's a hullabaloo?" asked the boy.

"A hubbub, a racket, a din," he said.

"We were just calling out for you so that you'd come," said the girl.

"Yes but, we don't want the whole world to hear you shouting 'wizard' at the top of your voices through the woods. People might begin to wonder why and become suspicious. Besides which, it's first thing in the morning and you are disturbing the dawn chorus," he said.

"What's the dawn chorus?" asked the boy.

"It's first thing in the morning when all the birds sing to each other because the insects they eat haven't woken up yet," explained the wizard.

They stopped there a moment and stood perfectly still and all listened to the birds singing from the branches of the trees. Their beautiful songs were swept along on the gentle morning wind, echoing through the wood, calling and replying to each other. It was a wonderful clear sunrise that morning, one the children would remember for a long time. Then their time alone was halted as they heard a dog barking in the distant woods somewhere.

"Dog walkers already, so early in the morning, they must like this time as much as I do. Come on, we must go. I will show you around the woods quickly before more come," said the wizard.

"We brought you some cake mister wizard," said the boy and he gave him a tin with it in.

The wizard opened the tin, looked at the cake and sniffed it then said, "Mmm chocolate cake is my favourite thank you very much. You can call me Wendell, which is my name; I'm Wendell the Wizard of Worsley Woods."

"Pleased to meet you Wendell, my name Jack," said the boy.

"And I'm Jill," said the girl.

"Jack and Jill, like in the nursery rhyme: Jack and Jill went up the hill to fetch a pale of water, Jack fell down and broke his crown and Jill came tumbling after," said the wizard.

"That rhyme is stupid, I mean what is a pail?" asked Jack.

"It means 'bucket'," said the wizard.

"And why would we go UP the hill to fetch some water? Wouldn't water have run down the hill and be at the bottom of it?" asked the girl.

"I suppose you're right," said the wizard.

"Also, if I fell down, why would I break my crown? Why was Jack wearing a crown? Was he a king or a prince?" asked Jack.

"I do not know, I didn't write the poem. Now we really must be getting going or soon the woods will be too busy for me," said the wizard and he took the children on a little tour to show them around the woods...

10. WORSELY WOODS

"This part of the woods where we met is called the High Woods because it is higher than the rest of the woods," said the wizard as he led them down the slope to the path by the swampy area of the brook. There they saw an old tree stump with coins stuck in to it.

"Why are there coins stuck in that tree stump?" asked Jack.

"That is a wishing tree, or what's left of it. People put coins in the tree and then make a wish in the hope that it will bring good luck," said the wizard.

"Does it work?" asked Jill.

"I don't know, I have never tried it," said the wizard.

Then he led them down the wood path to where the motorway tunnel was: one side of the tunnel was road and the other side was the brook.

"What is through that tunnel?" asked Jill.

"That goes to the North Woods; it runs along edge of the brook and it leads to Roe Green, where the deer live. If you cross the bridge over the brook that is on the other side and go left, that will lead you to the West Wood," explained the wizard.

"Which way are we going then?" asked Jack.

"Well we haven't got time to go everywhere today so we will go my way. Follow me children," said the wizard as he walked over the bridge just before the motorway tunnel.

Then on the other side of the bridge Robin Redbreast flew over and landed on the wizard's hat and the children laughed.

"Hello Robin Redbreast," said the wizard and the bird tweeted to him and he replied, "Oh it is OK. These children are my friends, they are Jack and Jill and I am showing them around the woods."

Then the little bird nodded at them both and flew off to look for grubs.

"Was that your friend?" asked Jill.

"Yes I am friends with all the animals, well nearly all of them. There are a few cows that don't like me and I had an argument with a fox last year, but apart from that I like all of nature. It is my job to look after the woods," said the wizard.

"The Wizard of Worsley Woods," said the children both at once.

"Do you want to hear a poem about me?" asked the wizard.

"Yes go on then," they replied.

So the wizard stood tall, and like an actor, took a large breath and began.

"I'm the Wizard of Worsley Woods
I only ever do good
And all the animals know my name
And far and wide they know my fame

I'm the Wizard of Worsley Woods
Help anyone one I could
I love the flowers and the trees
And all the birds and all the bees

I'm the Wizard of Worsley Woods
I'm never misunderstood
For I am magic and I am kind
I'm the nicest wizard you'll ever find

Because I'm...

The Wizard of Worsley Woods!"

When he finished the children clapped wholeheartedly.

"We had already heard that before, our grandma told it us," said Jill.

"Really? I wasn't aware of many other people who knew that. Anyway we must be getting on with our tour of the woods. We haven't got all day," said the wizard.

"We have got all day," said Jack.

"I haven't got all day. I am a busy man. I'm busier than a bee on a business trip," replied the wizard.

11. MOUSE & SQUIRREL

Over the little bridge they went and the path turned to the left and began to climb upwards. Up they went and as they did the muddy path became much drier and stonier. At the top of the path they came out at a large area of long grass pasture surrounded by a wooden fence that ran alongside the path.

"Windy Meadow," said the wizard.

"It's nice here," said Jack.

"My friend the Wise Owl lives in that tall tree over there," said the wizard pointing to a large tree by the edge of the field, "And my mouse friend lives somewhere around here," said the wizard pointing into the grass. Then he shouted out across the field, "Pipsqueak!"

He peered into the long grass and whistled. Out from the grass ran a tiny mouse that climbed up a post of the fence that ran around the side of the field. It squeaked towards the wizard and he took a nut from out of his pocket and gave to the little creature.

"Do you really know that mouse?" asked Jill curiously.

"Yes I do, his name is Pipsqueak," said the wizard. Then he turned to the mouse and spoke to it: "Hello Pipsqueak, tell me what you know."

Then the mouse squeaked at him while he listened.

"What did he tell you?" asked Jack.

"He said there has been a buzzard flying around here an hour ago but he never saw any owls in the night. Mice and birds don't really get along together too good," said the wizard.

"Ask him something else," said Jill.

"What is the weather going to be like today?" the wizard asked the mouse and it squeaked back at him.

"What did it say?" asked Jill.

"He said it would be raining by the evening. Mice can smell rain from a long way off," he explained.

Then he took them further down the path where they came to the grand gates of a large house that sat by the lake in the woods.

"Who lives in this huge house?" asked Jack.

"This is known as The Aviary. It is where the herons live. They are very posh and keep themselves to themselves," said the wizard.

"Can we meet them?" asked Jack.

"Oh no, they don't like visitors; they don't even wish to talk to me. We must leave the herons in peace. Even when they come down to the lake to concentrate on fishing they don't like to be talked to," he said.

After that they came to a road but soon turned off back into the wood, past an old stone that said 'Old Warke', and then down towards the brook that came from the bottom of Old Warke Dam. Next they went down to the Lower Brook that ran through the wood valley. Here they saw some squirrels scampering about busily digging in the earth.

"Hello there Thquirrel," the wizard said to one of them nearby.

The squirrel squeaked back.

"Ooh really," replied the wizard.

Then the squirrel squeaked some more and the wizard replied, "Oh really," again.

Jack and Jill looked puzzled.

"What is that squirrel saying to you?" asked Jill.

"His name is Thquirrel and he's saying he buried some nuts around here last autumn, but he can't find them because he has forgotten where he put them. For two weeks he and his cousins have been searching the whole area," explained the wizard.

Then he took a nut from out of his pocket and gave it to the squirrel who thanked him gladly.

"Good luck with your search," said the wizard and he walked off.

"Good luck," said Jack and Jill to the squirrel and it squeaked goodbye to them.

"Can you really talk to all the animals?" asked Jill.

"Yes, it's not that difficult if you put your mind to it," said the wizard.

"Can you teach us to speak cat?" asked Jack.

"Yes but not today, it would take some time," he replied.

"Our grandma has a cat called Mrs Chubbington and it's very old," said Jill.

"What a funny name for a cat," remarked the wizard.

"It's a very fat cat," added Jack.

"It never stops eating," said Jill.

"Well maybe another day I will teach you to talk cat," half-promised the wizard.

12. THE LAKE

From the brook valley bottom they climbed up the steps by the dam and turned left to see the full length of the lake.

"Beautiful isn't it," said the wizard, and it truly was. The sun sprinkled down through the leaves on to the water which was so still it looked like a mirror, reflecting the fine green trees and plants that grew around it. Morning mist rose up from the lake and on the grass edges sat the local ducks, sunbathing in the early morning sun, some yawning and some still sleeping.

"Grandma calls it Old Warke Dam," said Jack.

"I always thought the part that stopped the water was the 'dam' and the water was the lake," said the confused wizard.

Then they walked around the lake chatting and pointing at things. It had become a lovely fine morning.

"Just in case we bump into some early dog walkers we should tell them that I am not a real wizard, I'm just going to a fancy dress party," he said and Jack and Jill agreed it was a good idea.

Luckily they didn't meet any dog walkers or people in the wood and they soon came to the lake pier; a wooden walkway that went out over the water.

"This is where I come to feed the ducks, or as I like to call them 'The Quacklings'," said the wizard.

Then he took some bread from his pocket and began throwing it in the water. As he did this all the ducks came over to get some breakfast. They made a great kerfuffle as they squabbled with each other for the crumbs.

Then two majestic swans came gliding over the water towards them.

"Ah, here comes the Lord and Lady of the Lake," said the wizard.

"Are swans very posh?" asked Jack.

"Yes they are very aristocratic and well bred. Not like these common ducks scrabbling and splashing about. Swans move with elegance and grace," he said.

When he had run out of bread to give them they walked on from the pier, around to where an old house stood at the boggy end of the lake. The wizard put his fingers to his lips and went 'shhh'.

"This house is Badger's Lodge," whispered the wizard.

"Do badgers live in this house?" asked Jill.

"Not actually in it, but they live nearby at the end of the back garden in a badger set. So be very quiet when we pass," he said.

"Why do we have to be quiet?" asked Jack.

"Badgers are nocturnal, they are up awake all night looking for food, and in the day time they are fast asleep snoring," explained the wizard as they silently tip-toed past.

Then they finally got to the place where they had met at the High Woods. They had gone in a full circle. The morning was now bright and clear. Voices of walkers could be heard and a dog barked in the distance.

"I must be going now," said the wizard.

"Already?" asked Jack unhappily.

"People are up and about and I don't want to be seen," he explained.

"Yes we must go now Jack before someone sees him," said Jill.

"I have things to do; I need to go to the West Wood to see a bat with a sore ear," said the wizard.

"Can we come and see you again?" asked Jack.

"Yes I suppose so, but don't shout, whistle or something, and bring more cake," said the wizard.

Then he said goodbye and disappeared up the forest path and was gone, as if he had never been there at all.

13. THE TEA PARTY

From that day on Jack, Jill and the wizard became good friends. Every time they went to stay with their grandma, who lived by the woods, they went to see the wizard. He taught them about the woods and the plants and the animals that lived there. He showed them what an oak tree looked like, and a sycamore tree and a beech tree; their leaves and seeds. He told them about the woodland flowers and the blossoms and the seasons they bloom in. He told them about the fairies and bats that came out on midsummer nights. He also explained to them the importance of looking after nature and how good it feels to spend time walking in the woods.

Too soon the school holidays came to an end and they wouldn't be able to visit again until the end of term. Up until that point he had kept his home secret, but as he now trusted them, the wizard invited them to his tree house to have a tea party on their last day.

"If I let you come to my tree house will you promise never to tell anyone where I live?" the wizard asked them and they both agreed.

Then he led them through the woods and down a secret path that went round and around. He took them in circles and the

wrong way then the right way, until they couldn't properly remember which way they had come. So they just followed the wizard.

When they eventually got there they loved his tree house, especially the rope ladder, which could be pulled up to stop people getting in. They all climbed up and squeezed into his little home and sat around the table. There were other guests there too: a robin, an owl and a hedgehog.

"Let me introduce you to my friends," said the wizard. He pointed to the owl and said, "This is my dear friend Owlberta the Wise Owl, she has lived in these woods for longer than I can remember, but recently seems to have moved into my house."

Jack and Jill said 'hello' and the owl squawked back at them.

Next the wizard pointed to the robin and said, "This is my good friend Robin Redbreast, I see him nearly every day out and about in the woods."

Jack and Jill said 'nice to meet you' to the robin and it tweeted back to them.

After that the wizard pointed to the hedgehog and said, "This is Pricklebob, he is new to the woods. He only came here not long before I met you two."

Jack and Jill said 'hi' to the hedgehog and the hedgehog made a funny little squeaky hedgehog noise back to them.

The wizard could understand what the animals where saying but the children could not, so the wizard spent most of his time explaining to the children what the animals where saying.

Jack and Jill brought a chocolate cake and some scones and the wizard made a pot of tea. He said tea but, luckily for the children, it wasn't hot boring tea like their grandma drank. It was cold tea in a teapot with ice cubes, but it wasn't tea made with teabags, it was tea made with blackcurrant cordial, and it was exceedingly nice to drink, so much so that the wizard had to make several pots of it. The cake and scones were cut and shared out and they all had lovely time, even if it was a little cramped in the tree house.

The robin told a story about following a wild pig through the forest and getting lost. The hedgehog told them of his journey across the dangerous road to the wood. The owl told them about the time she tried to fly to the moon but before she was almost very nearly there, the sun rose in the morning and the moon vanished and she never made it. All of these stories had to be translated to Jack and Jill by the wizard, because they couldn't understand what the animals were saying.

Then the tea party ended. All the cake had been eaten and all the cold blackcurrant tea had been drank.

"Now it's getting late, it is time for everyone to go home. Jack and Jill you must be going to your grandma's house or she will be worrying about you. Robin Redbreast, you need to go and be with your family. Pricklebob the hedgehog, you have to go and find a nice hedge to live under and Owlberta the Wise Owl, you need to go back to your tree by the Windy Meadow. You have been living at my house for weeks, eating all my food and sitting on my comfy chair," said the wizard.

"But can't I stay a bit longer? I have been ill," said the owl.

"You haven't been ill for weeks, it's time you went before you overstayed your welcome," explained the wizard and the owl sadly agreed.

Then they left the tree house. Jack and Jill climbed down the rope ladder and the wizard went down carrying the hedgehog, because he couldn't get down himself. The robin flew off straight away and the owl reluctantly sat on the roof for a while flapping her wings before eventually she lazily glided off home.

The wizard went with the children to the edge of the wood and they all said goodbye.

"If we come again in the next school holidays can you take us to see some fairies?" asked Jill hopefully.

"Oh I don't know about that. The fairies don't like to be seen, even more so than me!" said the wizard.

"Oh please Wendell!" begged Jack.

"We will see, we will see," he said.

"When adults say 'we will see' it always means 'no'," said Jill.

"No it doesn't," said the wizard with a grin.

Then he walked off into the woods and disappeared.

14. THE UNEXPECTED CALL

The children started a new term at school and for weeks they didn't see the wizard at all, nor did they tell anyone else about him. They kept him secret from everyone, except their grandma of course. They told her everything about the wizard in the woods, so much so she had had to tell them to stop talking about him all the time.

Jack and Jill had been so busy at school that their friend Wendell the Wizard of Worsley Woods seemed like he had been a dream. They had to spend all their time reading and writing and doing maths they didn't get chance to go to see their grandma or the wizard.

Then one weekend, in the middle of term, their grandma phoned them up and asked them to come and visit her. She seemed very sad.

When they got there she told them that her cat, Mrs Chubbington, who was very fat and old, had fallen out of a tree after chasing a bird. It had broken its leg and was just sat in its basket sleeping and refusing to eat or move. She had told the vet to see the cat but the vet said the cat was too old to have an operation and there was nothing they could do. Grandma was awfully worried that her cat would die.

"But what can we do? We do not know how to make the cat better," Jill said to her grandma.

"I know you don't know what to do, but could you ask your wizard friend if he could help?" asked grandma.

"Yes he will be able to help," said Jack.

"But what if he can't help Mrs Chubbington? What if he won't come into the town, he doesn't like people seeing him," warned Jill.

"Just ask him, that's all you can do. It's my last chance to try and save my cat. Please just go and ask him," their grandma asked.

Jack and Jill went once again to the woods to search for the wizard. They stood in the High Woods and whistled and shouted for him but he did not come. Then they decided to go to his house to get him but they couldn't remember the way to it. They just went around and around in circles and couldn't find it.

"Oh it's no use, we can't find him," said Jack.

"His tree house must be about here somewhere. We need to find his secret path," said Jill.

Then a robin landed on a tree nearby and tweeted to them.

"Look Jill, its Robin Redbreast," said Jack.

Jill went over to the bird and said, "Please Robin Redbreast, can you show us the way to the wizard's tree house. We need to see him. It is very important!"

The little bird chirped back to her.

"What did it say?" asked Jack.

"I haven't got a clue, I don't speak robin," admitted Jill.

Luckily, the tiny bird could understand what she had said and it flew off a few yards up the path and tweeted to them, beckoning them to follow. They followed it. Then the bird flew on ahead of them and waited on branches for them to catch up and this way it led them to the path to the wizard's hidden tree house.

When they got there the rope ladder was pulled up. This meant the wizard was in. So they called up to him.

"Wendell!" shouted Jack.

"Wendell!" shouted Jill.

Then they heard some noise and the tree house began to shake. Then the door was flung open and the wizard poked his head out blinking.

"What's all the shouting? What's all the fuss? Why are you two here? Has term finished already?" asked the confused wizard.

"We need your help," said Jack.

"Our grandma needs your help," said Jill.

"Why, what is up with her?" he asked.

"It's not her, its Mrs Chubbington," explained Jack.

"Who is Mrs Chubbington? I don't know her?" replied the wizard.

"It's grandma's cat. It has fallen out of a tree and hurt itself so much it won't move and it has stopped eating," Jill told him.

"A cat that has stopped eating is a bad sign. Usually cats eat all the time," said the wizard.

"You look after all the other animals. We hoped you might be able to make the cat better," said Jill.

"Will you come into town to see her and make her well?" asked Jack.

"Come to town? Me? Town with other people in, I might get seen by someone," said the wizard looking nervous.

"If anyone sees you we will simply tell them you are on your way to a fancy dress party," said Jill.

"Oh I don't know. I feel very scared out in the town. There are too many people there," said the wizard.

"You'll be safe with us," said Jill.

"Please!" begged Jack.

"It isn't even that far from the wood. You probably won't meet anyone," said Jill.

"We will be there in five minutes," said Jack.

"It's not even a town, its a little housing estate," said Jill.

"Oh all right then, just this once. I am never going into the town ever again after this," agreed the wizard.

Then the wizard lowered the rope ladder from his tree house and climbed down. The children took him to grandma's house, on a little housing estate, which wasn't too far from the woods.

15. GRANDMA'S CAT

Luckily they weren't seen by anybody as they walked into town. When they arrived at grandma's house Mrs Chubbington was curled up in her basket, not moving nor eating, just letting out the occasional moan. It looked very sorry for itself. The wizard knelt down and asked her, "What seems to be the matter poor cat?"

The cat meowed back to him. Grandma and the children couldn't understand what the cat was saying but the wizard could.

"There was a pesky pigeon in the garden, so I chased it up the tree. Then I realised I was too old for climbing trees and I froze still. I sat on the branch very scared and decided to wait there until someone came and got me down," said the cat.

"Then what happened?" he asked.

"I waited for hours and no one came. Then the wind blew me off the branch and I fell to the ground. I have badly hurt my leg and I hurt all over. I feel like I am going to the great cat basket in the sky," said the cat.

"Well have you used up all of your nine lives? Everyone knows that cats have nine lives. Tell me how you lost all your other lives," said the wizard.

"My first life was lost when I was a kitten and I nearly got run over, then I fell in a pond and escaped. Then I fell in the same pond again and got dragged out by the scruff of my neck," said the cat.

"That's three lives," said the wizard.

"Then I got in a fight with a large dog, and then I ran under a bus, I fell down a sewer, got stung by a swarm of bees and fell out of the tree the other day," the cat told him.

"That's only eight lives gone."

"Is it?"

"Yes."

"I thought I had used up all my nine lives and I was done for," said the cat looking very surprised.

"No you have one life left. Now let me bandage your leg and give you some medicine," said the wizard and that is what he did.

After the treatment Mrs Chubbington started meowing for food. Grandma gave her a special treat of salmon, which cats love, and Mrs Chubbington ate it all down in one go.

"She certainly has got her appetite back Wendell," said grandma.

"She will be perfectly fine. She just needed a little chat and some medicine," said the wizard.

"What were you and the cat talking about?" asked Jill.

"I was just asking how many of her nine lives she had used up. Turns out she had one left and she was going to get better anyway," he said.

"Well thank you very much Wendell, to me you have saved my cat's life, whatever it was you did. Now if you ever need any cake, just come and ask me and I will bake you one whenever you like," said grandma.

"A cake whenever I want, even chocolate cake?" he asked in surprise.

"Yes, even chocolate cake. I want to repay you for your kindness," she said.

"Well it is my job to be kind to the animals. I am after all the Wizard of Worsley Woods," he said.

Then Jack and Jill and Grandma all together sang his rhyme to him and the wizard became rather shy but also proud of himself.

"The Wizard of Worsley Woods
He only ever does good
And all the animals know his name
And far and wide they know his fame

The Wizard of Worsley Woods
Helps anyone one he could
He loves the flowers and the trees
And all the birds and all the bees

The Wizard of Worsley Woods
Is never misunderstood
For he is magic and he is kind
The nicest wizard you'll ever find

Is...

The Wizard of Worsley Woods!"

Then the wizard said goodbye to them all
and went back to his tree house in the woods.

The End

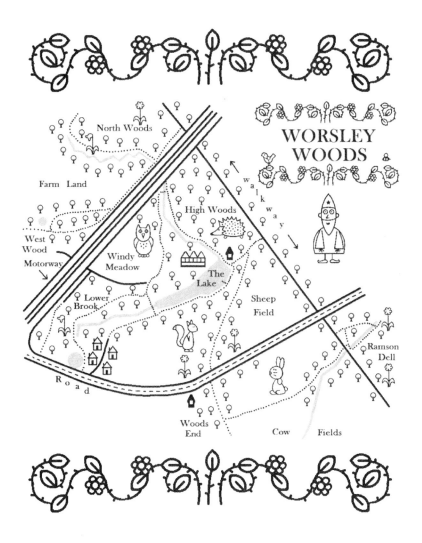

North Woods

WORSLEY
WOODS

Farm Land

High Woods

West
Wood

Motorway

walkway

Windy
Meadow

The
Lake

Sheep
Field

Lower
Brook

Ramson
Dell

Road

Woods
End

Cow   Fields

Printed in Great Britain
by Amazon

19868112R00051